A Very Proper Fox

For Emily, Olivia and Sophie

First published in paperback in Great Britain by HarperCollins Children's Books in 2006

1 3 5 7 9 10 8 6 4 2

ISBN-13: 978-0-00-787512-2

HarperCollins Children's Books is a division of HarperCollins Publishers Ltd.

Text and illustrations copyright © Jan Fearnley 2006

Visit our website at: www.harpercollins.co.uk

Printed and bound in China
Colour Reproduction by Dot Gradations Ltd, UK

A Very Proper Fox

Jan Fearnley

HarperCollins *Children's Books*

Every evening Frankie the Fox sat on his hill and watched the sunset. Sometimes, if the wind was in the right direction and if he listened very carefully, Frankie could hear the most beautiful song drifting across the valley.

Whenever Frankie heard the sweet music, it filled his heart with joy. He couldn't help himself—he danced and danced and danced.

One night, Naughty Rabbit popped out
of his burrow and said, "What sort of a crazy,
dancing fox are you? Proper foxes don't jig
about. Proper foxes catch chickens."

"Don't they catch rabbits too?" asked Frankie.

"Oh, no, no, nooo!" said Rabbit. "Boy, you've
got a lot to learn."

"Foxes catch chickens," insisted Rabbit. "And I know where there's a BIG FAT JUICY one, just across the valley. A PROPER fox would go and get it!"

Frankie desperately wanted to be a proper fox. Off he went to catch the chicken.

Naughty Rabbit smiled wickedly.

He didn't like chickens.

He liked causing trouble.

Frankie stole down the lane
to the chicken's house.
He licked his lips,
flexed his claws,
growled like a proper fox,
low and mean...
"I'M COMING TO GET YOU!"

But instead of a big,
fat chicken, Frankie
found a big, fat mess!
A rickety fence with the
paint peeling off. A gate
hanging from its hinges.

"What a shambles!"
Frankie said.
"I'd better sort
this out."

Frankie hammered and
painted until everything
was fixed.

He couldn't help it.
He was a very
tidy fox.

It was very late when he'd finished. Frankie was
too tired to catch a chicken. He went home
for a rest, and beans on toast.

Rabbit wanted some beans too.
"I hope you'll do better next time!" he said.

The next night, Frankie set out with
Rabbit's words ringing in his ears
and evil intent in his heart.
He licked his lips,
flexed his claws,
growled like a proper fox,
low and mean...
"I'M COMING TO GET YOU!"

But all he found
was a terrible mess.
"What a dump!"

Chick Peas

Cock-a-Doodle
NOODLES

WAKEY*WAKEY
CORNFLAKES

Frankie washed
and scrubbed until
everything sparkled.

He couldn't help it.
He was a very
tidy fox.

When he was finished,
it was far too late for
anything energetic, like
catching chickens.

Once again, Frankie trundled
home for beans on toast.
Once again, Rabbit had
plenty to say.

"What a shameful display of incompetence!
Proper foxes are supposed to eat chickens,
not iron their knickers! Get that
bird tonight, or ELSE!"

That night, Frankie was determined.

He licked his lips, like a proper fox...

"I'M COMING TO GET YOU..."

He flexed his claws, like a proper fox...

"I'M COMING TO GET YOU..."

He growled his growl, like a proper fox...

"I'M COMING TO GET YOU...

...as soon as I've watered these poor, thirsty flowers and sorted out this garden!"

Frankie worked harder than ever. Soon he was utterly exhausted.

He sat down for a little rest and fell fast asleep in among the pumpkins.

The next morning, Frankie awoke to sunshine and the sound of beautiful music. It was the chicken, singing his favourite song!

This was his chance... to get her!

Frankie licked his lips, flexed his claws, leapt up...

...and danced **and danced and danced.**

He couldn't help it!

The chicken stopped singing and regarded Frankie
with a cool eye. "I want a word with you," she said.
"Are you the one who mended my fence? Who
tidied my house and watered my tomatoes?"
Frankie nodded – sheepishly.

"Then you had better come in."

Frankie and the chicken, who was called Madame Mimi, took tea together.

Over buttery crumpets, they got to know each other.

Over chocolate cake, they became friends.

Madame Mimi was a singer in the opera.

Her clever little eyes twinkled as she listened to Frankie's story – especially the bits about grabbing chickens!

She was a very busy (and messy) lady, but not too busy to notice Frankie's kindness.

"Call me crazy," she said, "but I have an idea."

Madame Mimi invited
Frankie to come and live with her.
"I'll never be a proper fox now," chuckled Frankie.

"Who cares!" clucked the feathery diva.
"You are perfect as you are. You are a proper
friend, and that is all that matters."

Mimi taught
Frankie to sing.

He made a very
fine baritone.

Frankie taught Mimi tidiness – and some nifty dance moves!

Maybe it was crazy; a fox and a chicken together, but Frankie and Mimi were very happy.

They made beautiful music together,
and tasty beans on toast.

And as for Naughty Rabbit...

...he slunk away quietly one night.
Apparently, a little bird told Frankie that proper
foxes DO eat rabbits. And the tastiest ones of all
are the naughty ones that like to stir up trouble.